ALPINE SKIING

THE STORY OF CANADIANS IN THE OLYMPIC WINTER GAMES

Written by Blaine Wiseman

Weigl

Published by Weigl Educational Publishers Limited
6325 10 Street SE
Calgary, Alberta
T2H 2Z9

www.weigl.com

Library and Archives Canada Cataloguing in Publication data available upon request.
Fax 403-233-7769 for the attention of the Publishing Records department.

ISBN 978-1-55388-948-9 (hard cover)
ISBN 978-1-55388-957-1 (soft cover)

Printed in the United States of America
1 2 3 4 5 6 7 8 9 0 13 12 11 10 09

Editor: Heather C. Hudak
Design: Terry Paulhus

All of the Internet URLs given in the book were valid at the time of publication. However, due to the dynamic nature of the Internet, some addresses may have changed, or sites may have ceased to exist since publication. While the author and publisher regret any inconvenience this may cause readers, no responsibility for any such changes can be accepted by either the author or the publisher.

Every reasonable effort has been made to trace ownership and to obtain permission to reprint copyright material. The publishers would be pleased to have any errors or omissions brought to their attention so that they may be corrected in subsequent printings.

Weigl acknowledges Getty Images as its primary image supplier for this title.

We gratefully acknowledge the financial support of the Government of Canada through the Book Publishing Industry Development Program (BPIDP) for our publishing activities.

Contents

What are the Olympic Winter Games?

The Olympic Games began more than 2,000 years ago in the town of Olympia in Ancient Greece. The Olympics were held every four years in August or September and were a showcase of **amateur** athletic talent. The games continued until 393 AD, when they were stopped by the Roman emperor.

The Olympics were not held again for more than 1,500 years. In 1896, the first modern Olympics took place in Athens, Greece. The games were the idea of Baron Pierre de Coubertin of France. Though they did not feature any winter sports, in later years, sports such as ice skating and ice hockey were played at the Olympics.

In 1924, the first Olympic Winter Games were held at Chamonix, France. The Games featured 16 nations, including Canada, the United States, Finland, France, and Norway. There were 258 athletes competing in 16 events, which included skiing, ice hockey, and speed skating. The first gold medal in a winter sport was awarded to speed skater Charles Jewtraw of the United States in the 500-metre event.

Today, alpine skiing is featured in 10 different events at the Winter Olympic Games. There are five women's **disciplines** and five men's disciplines in alpine skiing. They are downhill, slalom, giant slalom, Super G, and Super Combined. The rules for men's and women's events are the same, but the courses are different sizes. Some of the best alpine skiing nations are Canada, the United States, Austria, Germany, France, Switzerland, and Norway.

TOP 10 MEDAL-WINNING COUNTRIES	
COUNTRY	MEDALS
Norway	280
United States	216
USSR	194
Austria	185
Germany	158
Finland	151
Canada	119
Sweden	118
Switzerland	118
Democratic Republic of Germany	110

CANADA 119

UNITED STATES 216

CANADIAN TIDBIT Vancouver will be the third Canadian city to host the Olympic Games. Montreal hosted the Summer Games in 1976, and Calgary hosted the Winter Games in 1988.

Winter Olympic Sports

Currently, there are seven Olympic winter sports, with a total of 15 disciplines. All 15 disciplines are listed here. In addition, there are five Paralympic Sports. These are alpine skiing, cross-country skiing, **biathlon**, ice sledge hockey, and wheelchair curling.

Alpine Skiing

Biathlon

Bobsleigh

Cross-Country Skiing

Curling

Figure Skating

Freestyle Skiing

Ice Hockey

Luge

Nordic Combined

Short Track Speed Skating

Skeleton

Ski Jumping

Snowboarding

Speed Skating

FINLAND 151

SWEDEN 118

USSR 194

NORWAY 280

GERMANY 158

DEMOCRATIC REPUBLIC OF GERMANY 110

SWITZERLAND 118

AUSTRIA 185

Canadian Olympic Alpine Skiing

Anne Heggtveit also competed in the giant slalom and downhill events, finishing 12th in both.

People first began skiing thousands of years ago in **Scandinavia**. Alpine skiing also was very important to people in the European Alps. They lived in mountainous areas and used skis to move downhill, as well as across flat terrain. Skis were used to quickly move across the snow for hunting and transportation. In the 19th century, when Europeans began moving to Canada, they brought skiing with them. In the Rocky Mountains of British Columbia and Alberta, skiing became a popular pastime with the many Norwegian immigrants.

Canada first took part in alpine skiing at the 1936 Winter Olympics. It was represented by seven skiers but did not win any medals. The country's first alpine skiing medal came 20 years later, in 1956. Lucille Wheeler finished third place, winning a bronze medal in the women's downhill event at Cortina, Italy. Four years later, Anne Heggtveit became the first Canadian alpine skier to win a gold medal at the Olympics, finishing first in the slalom event.

At the 1968 Olympics in Grenoble, France, Canada had its best alpine skiing performance. Nancy Greene won gold medals in giant slalom and combined, as well as a silver medal in slalom. Greene's performance was the best by a female alpine skier at any Olympics until Croatia's Janica Kostelic won three gold medals and one silver during the 2002 Games.

At the 1976 Winter Olympics, 18-year-old Kathy Kreiner of Canada (centre) became the youngest skier up to that date to win an Olympic gold medal.

At the 1992 Winter Olympics, Kerrin Lee-Gartner celebrated her gold medal win.

In 1968, Nancy Greene won a gold medal in the giant slalom in Grenoble, France.

In 1980, Canada won its first medal in a men's Olympic alpine skiing event. That year, a group of Canadian skiers, known as the "Crazy Canucks," wanted to make Canada an international skiing power. Although they had won several international competitions, all but one were disappointed at the 1980 Olympics. Steve Podborski took the bronze in downhill, winning the first-ever medal by a male Canadian alpine skier.

In 1988, Karen Percy won two bronze medals in front of her hometown crowd in Calgary, Alberta. Finishing third in both the downhill and the Super G competitions, Percy brought Canadian women back into the spotlight in alpine skiing. At the following Olympics, Kerrin Lee-Gartner continued the success of past Canadian women's alpine skiers by winning gold in the downhill.

In 1994, Canadian Edi Podivinsky won an alpine skiing medal. Though this is the most recent alpine skiing win for Canada, a new generation of skiers, both male and female, hope to bring Canada back to the podium at future Olympics.

♦ **CANADIAN TIDBIT** Karen Percy is married to former NHL hockey player Kevin Lowe. Lowe has worked for the Canadian men's hockey team as an assistant executive director at both the 2002 and 2006 Winter Olympics.

All The Right Equipment

Alpine skiers glide down snow-covered hills on two skis, using two poles to help push them along. Specialized equipment helps alpine skiers move down the hill as fast as possible.

Skis are two long, slim boards that are strapped to a person's feet. By distributing the weight of the person wearing them, skis allow skiers to stay on top of the snow, instead of sinking or falling through. In the past, skis were made from planks of wood. Today, they are made of lightweight materials, such as fibreglass, and have metal edges that dig into the snow when the skier turns.

Alpine skis are wider than **nordic** skis, because alpine skiers must be able to turn much faster. Wider skis can handle more force when the skier digs the edges into the snow to turn. The skis are built extra strong to withstand the force of landing huge jumps at high speeds.

Although alpine skis are built strong, they must be flexible. Alpine skiers travel downhill at more than 100 kilometres per hour, twisting, turning, and flying through the air. Their skis must be able to twist and flex with the changing terrain and the stress of so much speed and movement.

Skiers wear special, sturdy boots that protect their feet from extreme conditions. The boot is attached to the ski at both the toe and heel with a device called a binding.

POLES

SKIS

AERODYNAMIC SUIT

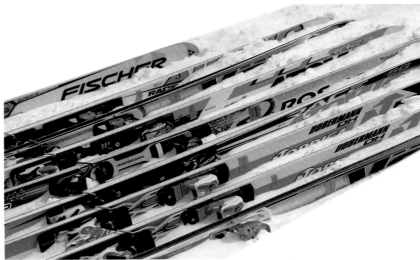

Athletes wear skis that are fitted to their height and body shape.

Alpine skiers use poles to help them explode out of the starting gates at the top of the mountain. Along the race course, the poles are used for turning and balance. Before the 1850s, skiers used one wooden pole to help push themselves along. The pole was long and could be used to push on both sides of the skier's body. Today, two poles are used to allow skiers to push themselves along more efficiently. Like skis, poles are made of lightweight, sturdy materials. This allows skiers to use the maximum amount of strength when pushing without breaking their equipment.

Alpine skiing is a winter sport that is performed outside, so skiers must wear clothing that protects them from cold weather. Olympic skiers wear tight-fitting, **aerodynamic** suits that reduce air resistance and keep them warm in cold weather.

Poles   Boots   Gloves   Goggles and Helmet

🍁 **CANADIAN TIDBIT** In 2007, the number of Canadian alpine skiers training for international competition grew to a record 55.

Qualifying to Compete

Skiers qualify for the Olympics by winning, or finishing well, in selection trials.

Reaching the Olympics is a difficult task for an alpine skier. A skier must complete several criteria before he or she will be allowed to compete as an Olympian.

Unlike other competitions, which have a certain number of places available, alpine skiing has an ideal number of 270 athletes competing. This means that there could be more or less than 270 skiers in the field. The places available are divided among the competing nations, which then select skiers to represent them at the Olympics. Only four skiers can compete for a country in each event. Canada can send a total of 22 alpine skiers to the Olympics. The team must be made up of men and women, with no more than 14 of either gender.

Skiers must perform well in the season leading up to the Olympics if they want to compete in the games. The top 500 skiers in the International Ski Federation (FIS) the year before the Olympics qualify to take part in the events. This number is much larger than the number of athletes allowed to compete in the Olympics, so each country picks its top-ranked skiers to participate in the Olympics.

Qualifying for the Canadian Olympic team takes a great deal of practice and hard work. Skiers must perform at a high level and show their dedication to success if they want to be chosen to compete in the Games.

Erik Guay won the men's downhill race of the Alpine Skiing World Cup in 2007.

Michaela Dorfmeister of Austria won the gold medal in the women's Super-G alpine skiing final at the 2006 Winter Olympic Games.

JUDGING

At Olympic alpine skiing competitions, there are several groups of officials that work together to ensure that racers follow the rules. Each performs specific duties that help the competition run smoothly.

A group of officials representing the FIS makes sure that the competition is prepared and executed properly. These officials include jury members, a race director, two referees, as well as a technical delegate and an assistant. The technical delegate is the highest official, making sure all aspects of the event are properly organized. The jury ensures that the event is performed according to FIS rules. It has the job of cancelling a race if the weather is too cold or determining if a competitor should

be disqualified. Jury members make decisions by voting on any issues that arise.

The start referee determines if a skier commits a false start. The finish referee makes sure that all rules are being followed at the finish line and that the competition is timed properly. A different team of officials is in charge of timing the skiers.

Rules of Alpine Skiing

In Olympic alpine skiing competitions, men and women compete to ski down a hill in the fastest possible time. Each event presents different obstacles and challenges to the skiers, but the goal is always the same. Skiers must pass through a series of gates while skiing downhill until they reach the finish line. Each event has a different number of gates, and the way the gates are placed on the hill is different as well.

In the downhill event, athletes ski down the hill as fast as they can, making long, sweeping turns and using jumps to launch themselves through the air. The gates in this event are placed at least 8 metres apart, which gives the skiers room to maneuver at high speeds. The speed of downhill makes it a dangerous sport. Skiers must be highly skilled and athletic to stay in control and avoid crashing.

In the slalom event, there are more gates than in downhill, and they are placed much closer together. Skiers must weave between the gates, turning often. The gates used in slalom are flexible poles.

At the 2006 Winter Olympics, Ted Ligety of the United States skied the slalom run at Sestriere Colle, Sestriere, Italy.

🍁 **CANADIAN TIDBIT** In all alpine events, skiers can be penalized for missing a gate. Depending on the event, this can mean that time is added to their finishing time or they can be disqualified from the event.

Skiers use the edges of their skis to make sharp turns around the narrow gates. Skiers often touch the gates as they pass, making the sharpest turns possible.

Competitors wear shin guards, padded gloves, and helmets as they carve around the gates.

Giant slalom is a similar event to slalom. Skiers make tight turns, weaving through gates. However, giant slalom uses more gates on a shorter course. In the Olympics, there can be as many as 70 gates.

The Super G event is a mix of downhill and giant slalom. The name stands for "super giant slalom." Skiers race as fast as they can downhill, while making sharp turns around flexible gates. The combination of these two events makes Super G very fast and technical.

Super combined features skiers competing in a mix of downhill and slalom events. Each skier does one downhill and two slalom runs. The skier with the fastest combined speed from all three runs is the winner.

PERFORMANCE ENHANCING DRUGS

Although the Olympics are a celebration of excellence and sportsmanship, some athletes use performance enhancing drugs to given them an unfair advantage over other athletes. There are many different types of performance enhancing drugs, including steroids. Some make muscles bigger, others help muscles recover more quickly, while some can make athletes feel less pain, giving them more **endurance**. The International Olympic Committee (IOC) takes the use of performance enhancing drugs very seriously. Regular testing of athletes helps ensure competitors do not use drugs to unnaturally improve their skills. Alpine skiing requires a mixture of strength, speed, and endurance. Many performance enhancing drugs will help an athlete in one of these areas, but hurt them in others. For example, a drug may cause the heart to pump more blood to muscles in the arms, making the athlete physically stronger. This takes blood away from the heart and lungs, giving the athlete less endurance and slower long-term recovery. There are serious mental and physical health problems that arise from using these drugs, such as sleep problems, sickness, and high blood pressure. Athletes who use steroids for a long time may die early from heart attacks and other problems.

Exploring the Venue

Whistler is ranked as the number one ski resort in North America.

Olympic events are held in specially built venues around the host city. These buildings can be used to exhibit one event or several, and can cost more than $1 billion to build.

Alpine skiing events at the 2010 Olympic Winter Games will be held at Whistler Creekside, a world-class ski hill in Whistler, British Columbia. More than 7,000 fans will attend Olympic alpine skiing events at this venue. The venue hosts millions of visitors every year, including many international skiing events.

CEREMONIES

Two of the most-anticipated and popular events of the Olympics are the opening and closing ceremonies. These events are traditionally held in the largest venue that an Olympic host city can offer. Facilities such as football, baseball, or soccer stadiums are often used for these events. At the 2008 Olympic Games in Beijing, more than 90,000 people attended the opening ceremonies. The ceremonies are spectacular displays that include music, dancing, acrobatic stunts, and fireworks. The theme of the ceremonies usually celebrates the history and culture of the host nation and city. All of the athletes participating in the Olympics march into the stadium during the ceremonies. The athletes wave their country's flag and celebrate the achievement of competing in the Olympics.

Whistler Mountain has hosted 11 FIS World Cup races since 1975.

There are two different courses used for the alpine skiing events in Whistler. Women's events are held on Franz's Run, while men's events take place on the Dave Murray Downhill. Each hill contains different combinations of turns, jumps, and other obstacles. The distance that women skiers cover ranges from 140 to 800 metres, depending on the event. Male competitors cover 180 to 1100 metres.

After the Games, Whistler Creekside will be used as a recreational ski hill, a training centre for the Canadian alpine ski team, and a competition venue for international events. Since Whistler Creekside was already built, it only needed to be upgraded for the Olympics. Upgrades to the facility cost $27.6 million

CANADIAN TIDBIT The Olympic Stadium in Montreal is one of the most expensive stadiums ever built. By the time it was paid off in 2006, the building had cost more than $1.4 billion.

COURSES FOR DIFFERENT EVENTS

MEN'S DOWNHILL START

CLOCK

The clock is triggered when the racer's shin hits a pivoting bar as he leaves the starting gate.

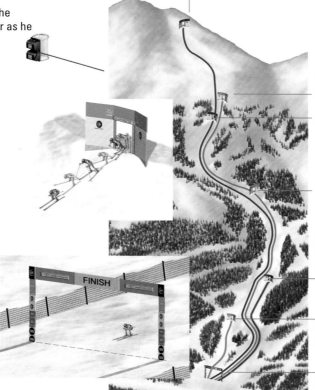

WOMEN'S DOWNHILL START

MEN'S SUPER-G START

WOMEN'S SUPER-G START

MEN'S AND WOMEN'S GIANT SLALOM START

MEN'S AND WOMEN'S SLALOM START

FINISH

START

After receiving the signal from the starting judge, the competitor has between 5 and 10 seconds to leave the starting gate, depending on the discipline. The skier gets an explosive start by pushing off hard with his poles, which he plants in front of the starting gate. The skier attempts to pick up as much speed as possible in the first few meters by using skating steps and pushing off with his poles.

FINISH LINE

Runs are timed to the tenth of a second. Time differences between competitors are very small.

OFFICIALS

Each event is run by an organizing committee and supervised by a competition jury made up of technicians, each of whom is responsible for different regulatory aspects of the competition. The clock tower and scoreboard are located at the bottom of the hill.

DOWNHILL, GIANT SLALOM, OR SUPER GIANT SLALOM

SLALOM TYPE TURNS

To perform a slalom type turn, the skier must be in a standing position with his or her knees slightly bent to act as a shock absorber, and the feet held close together. The turn is very dynamic, with little amplitude. The objective is to change direction quickly in order to negotiate the narrow slalom gates.

GIANT SLALOM-TYPE TURN

Also used in downhill and in Super-G, the skier makes this turn with his knees bent, chest slightly forward, and feet and arms apart. The weight is kept on the inside edge of the outside ski. The inside ski is mainly used to maintain balance. The aim is to execute the turns at maximum speeds. The skier uses the entire length of the ski edge to execute a strong carving turn.

POLES

These are used mainly to guide the turn and help the skier maintain his or her balance. They are curved, and offer minimal wind resistance when the skier assumes the tuck position. They are light and rigid, and are made from aluminum or composite fibers.

HELMET

The helmet is mandatory for speed events, and is worn by most skiers for all disciplines.

SUIT

The suit is form-fitted, and made from synthetic fibers. It offers a good air penetration coefficient while giving the skier complete freedom of movement.

Olympic Legends

Nancy Greene

Nancy Greene of Rossland, British Columbia, is known as Canada's greatest Olympic skier. Greene competed at the 1960 and 1964 Winter Olympics before achieving her Olympic dream in 1968 in Grenoble, France.

In 1967, Greene won the first-ever World Cup of alpine skiing. Although she had never finished higher than 7th place at the Olympics, Greene had her sights set high in 1968. In her first event, downhill, Greene finished tenth. In her next event, slalom, Greene won the silver medal. She won a gold medal in the last Olympic race of her career, the giant slalom. She carved her way down the hill in a time of 1 minute and 59.7 seconds. Greene's time was so fast that she beat the silver medallist by a record 2.67 seconds.

After retiring from competitive skiing, Greene has helped with the development of ski tourism in British Columbia and works at the Sun Peaks Ski Resort near Kamloops. In 2009, Greene entered politics, becoming a senator for her province. Greene's impact on skiing has been so great that she has had a skiing league named after her.

FAST FACT

• Greene's Canadian record of 13 World Cup victories still stands today.
• In November 1999, Nancy Greene was named Canada's female athlete of the century.

OLYMPIC MEDALS WON

1 Gold   1 Silver

Kerrin Lee-Gartner

In 1992, in Albertville, France, Kerrin Lee-Gartner of Trail, British Columbia, became the only Canadian to win an Olympic gold medal in downhill.

Lee-Gartner joined the Canadian national ski team when she was 16 years old. Concentrating on events that require a great amount of speed, she was often injured during the early part of her career. Lee-Gartner's injuries were so severe that she had both knees completely rebuilt. She persevered through the injuries and competed in her first Olympics in 1988, in Calgary, Alberta. Although she finished in 15th place, she knew that she could improve and was driven to be a champion.

The 1992 Olympics gave Lee-Gartner the chance she had been seeking. She skied the race of her life in Albertville and became a Canadian Olympic legend. Since retiring after the 1994 Olympic Winter Games, Lee-Gartner has worked as a broadcaster, covering Olympic and World Cup skiing events.

FAST FACT

Kerrin Lee-Gartner stands as the only Canadian ski racer, man or woman, to win Olympic gold in the downhill event.

OLYMPIC MEDALS WON

1 Gold

Anne Heggtveit

Anne Heggtveit began skiing in her hometown of Ottawa, Ontario, when she was two years old. She excelled at skiing and was winning tournaments by the age of seven. When she was only nine years old, Heggtveit was chosen as a member of the Canadian national ski team. This training helped Heggtveit prepare for her future as an Olympian.

At her first Olympics, in 1956, Heggtveit finished in 15th place in the slalom event. She continued training for the next four years and was ready to challenge the world's top skiers in 1960.

At the Winter Olympics in Squaw Valley, California, Heggtveit had the best performance of her career. She won the gold medal in slalom by finishing 3.3 seconds ahead of the silver medallist. In the history of Olympic slalom, there has not been a bigger time difference between first and second place.

FAST FACT

Anne Heggtveit was inducted into the Canadian Olympic Hall of Fame in 1971.

OLYMPIC MEDALS WON

1 Gold

Jean-Claude Killy

In the year leading up to the 1968 Olympics, France's Jean-Claude Killy won 12 of 16 World Cup races, completely dominating the international circuit. At the time, there were only three events in the men's Olympic alpine skiing competition. These events were downhill, slalom, and giant slalom. Killy's international success made him the favourite to win all three events at the Olympics in Grenoble, France.

In downhill, Killy managed to speed down the slope and win by only 8/100 of a second. In slalom, Killy won easily, claiming his second gold medal of the games. Killy skied well on both of his giant slalom runs and was in first place, until his rival, Karl Schranz of Austria, stopped skiing during his second run. Schranz claimed that someone had run across the foggy course, causing him to stop for safety reasons. The jury granted Schranz another run. On his rerun, Schranz beat Killy's time to win the gold medal. Later, the jury disqualified Schranz and gave the gold medal to Killy.

FAST FACT

Jean-Claude Killy was the second skier in Olympic history to sweep all three medals gold medals at the alpine events.

OLYMPIC MEDALS WON

3 Gold

WANT MORE?

Find out more about Anne Heggtveit at **www.skimuseum.ca/biodata.php?lang=en&id=48**.

For information about the Nancy Greene Ski League, visit **http://nancygreeneskileague.com**.

Olympic Stars

Erik Guay

Erik Guay, who lives and trains at Mont Tremblant, Quebec, has been skiing competitively since he was five years old. Having a ski coach for a father and a ski instructor for a mother helped Guay develop his skills at a young age. He began serious training when he was 12 years old, and in 1998, at the age of 17, Guay joined the Canadian national alpine ski team.

In 2007, Guay won his first World Cup event. That year, he finished in third place overall on the World Cup downhill circuit. This result gave Guay the confidence to compete with the best skiers in the world as part of Canada's Olympic team in 2010.

Manuel Osborne-Paradis

Vancouver's Manuel Osborne-Paradis has his hopes set on winning an Olympic gold medal on his home ski hill in Whistler in 2010.

At his first Olympics in 2006, Manuel Osborne-Paradis finished in 13th place in the downhill event. Since then, he has been rising up the charts in World Cup skiing.

In 2009, he won his first World Cup race in Norway. Two days later, he finished the weekend in third place on the same hill.

Britt Janyk

Before her 11th season as a member of the Canadian alpine ski team in 2006, Britt Janyk was told that she could remain on the team only if she paid for her own season. The cost was about $25,000. If she was able to qualify for the World Championships that year, the team would give her back 80 percent of the money. Janyk raised the money, and she went on to have her best season as a ski racer.

Janyk qualified for the World Championships, and she finished in fourth place, her best finish ever to that point. Janyk was given back most of her money and was allowed to compete on the team the following year.

Janyk had an even better year in 2007 to 2008. Only a week after winning her first medal, a bronze, in World Cup downhill, Janyk won a gold medal by finishing first in Aspen, Colorado. It was the first gold medal for a Canadian woman on the World Cup circuit in 15 years. She finished the season in third place overall.

Emily Brydon

Emily Brydon of Fernie, British Columbia, will compete in her third Winter Olympics in 2010. The nine-time Canadian champion has been a member of the Canadian alpine ski team since 1997, and has had to deal with serious injuries during her career. The speed and danger that come with alpine skiing have resulted in Brydon having surgery to repair both of her knees. She has fought through these injuries to win two World Cup gold medals.

WANT MORE?

Find out more about Canada's alpine ski team at **www.canski.org/webconcepteur/web/alpine/skiteam**.

For more about Canadian alpine skiers, visit **www.ctvolympics.ca/alpine-skiing/news/newsid=10609.html**.

A Day in the Life of an Olympic Athlete

Becoming an Olympic athlete takes a great deal of dedication and **perseverance**. Athletes must concentrate on remaining healthy and maximizing their strength and energy. Eating special foods according to a strict schedule, taking vitamins, waking up early to train and practise, and going to bed at a reasonable hour are important parts of staying in shape for world-class athletes. All athletes have different routines and training regimens. These regimens are suited to that athlete's body and lifestyle.

Eggs are a great source of **protein** and **iron**, and are low in **calories**, making them a popular breakfast choice. A cup of orange juice is a healthy breakfast drink, while coffee can give an athlete some extra energy in the morning. A light lunch, including a sandwich, yogurt, fruit, and juice, is usually a good option. This gives the body the right amount of energy, while it is not too filling. Chicken and pasta are popular dinnertime meals.

Athletes, such as Canada's Shona Rubens, Brigitte Acton, and Genevieve Simard, train hard to become skilled at their sport.

Early Mornings

Olympic athletes might wake up at 6:30 a.m. to record their resting **heart rate**. Next, they might stretch or perform yoga while their breakfast is preparing. The first exercise of the day can happen before 7:00 a.m. Depending on an athlete's sport, the exercise routine can vary. A skier might be in the gym lifting weights. After lifting weights for an hour, the athlete may move on to **aerobics** to help with strength and endurance.

6:30 a.m.

Morning Practice

By about 9:30 a.m., athletes are ready to practise their event. For a skier, this means hitting the slopes. Most Olympic athletes have coaches and trainers who help them develop training routines. After practice, skiers stretch to keep their muscles loose and avoid injuries. Many athletes use a sauna or an ice bath to help their muscles recover quickly.

9:30 a.m.

Afternoon Nap

At about noon, many athletes choose to take a break. Sleep helps the body and mind recover from stress. After waking up at 2:00 p.m., it is time for lunch and then, more exercise. **Core** exercises using special equipment help skiers with stability. Working out the leg muscles is an important part of training for skiers.

12:00 p.m.

Dinnertime

After the afternoon workout, it is dinnertime. Another healthy meal helps athletes recover from the day and prepare their body for the next day's training. The evening can be spent relaxing and doing some more light stretches. It is important for athletes to rest after a hard day of training so that they can do their challenging routine again the next day.

6:00 p.m.

Olympic Volunteers

Volunteers are an important part of creating an enjoyable Olympic experience for athletes and spectators. Thousands of volunteers help organize and execute the Olympic Games. Olympic volunteers are enthusiastic, committed, and dedicated to helping welcome the world to the host city. Volunteers help prepare for the Olympics in the years leading up to the events and even after the Olympics are over.

Potential volunteers are encouraged to get involved in the many sporting events that will be hosted at the Olympics.

The call for 25,000 volunteers for the 2010 Olympics in Vancouver was launched on February 12, 2008.

Before the Olympics begin, many countries send representatives to the host city to view event venues and plans. Olympic volunteers help make the representatives' stay enjoyable. From meeting these representatives at the airport, showing them around the city and the surrounding areas, and providing accommodations and transportation, volunteers make life easier for visitors to the host city.

✤ **CANADIAN TIDBIT** About 25,000 volunteers are helping with the Olympics in Vancouver. They will make sure the games are a memorable, enjoyable experience for athletes, judges, spectators, and officials from all over the world.

During the Olympics, volunteers help in many different areas. During the opening, closing, and medals ceremonies, volunteers help with costumes, props, and performers during the opening, closing. Editorial volunteers help by preparing written materials for use in promoting events and on the official website of the host Olympics. Food and beverage volunteers provide catering services to athletes, judges, officials, spectators, and media.

Some volunteers get a chance to view events and work with competitors. Anti-doping volunteers notify athletes when they have been selected for drug testing. These volunteers explain the process to the athletes and escort them to the drug-testing facility. Other volunteers get to be involved with the sporting events by helping to maintain the venues and the fields of play, providing medical assistance to athletes, transporting athletes to events, and helping with the set-up and effective running of events.

The Vancouver 2010 Olympic Torch Relay will be the longest relay held within the host country in history.

Torch Relay

One of the most anticipated events of each Olympics is the torch relay. The torch is lit during a ritual in Olympia, Greece, before it is flown to the host nation. The torch is then carried along a route across the country until it reaches the host city during the opening ceremonies. The torch relay for 2010 covers 45,000 kilometres over 106 days. The relay will begin in Victoria before moving through communities in all 10 Canadian provinces and three territories. About 12,000 volunteers will be chosen to carry the torch across Canada. Other volunteers help drive and maintain the vehicles that accompany the torch on its journey.

What are the Paralympics?

First held in 1960, the Paralympic Games are a sports competition for disabled competitors. Like the Olympics, the Paralympics celebrate the athletic achievements of its competitors. The Paralympics are held in the same year and city as the Olympics. Many sports appear in both the Paralympics and the Olympics, such as swimming, nordic skiing, and alpine skiing. The Paralympics also feature wheelchair basketball, **goalball**, and ice sledge hockey. The first Winter Paralympic Games were held in 1976.

Athletes competing at the Paralympics are classified by disability in six categories, including **amputee**, **cerebral palsy**, **visual impairment**, **spinal cord** injuries, **intellectual disability**, and a group for other disabilities. These classifications allow athletes to compete in a fair and equal basis in each event. Goalball, for example, is a sport for the visually impaired, and not for amputees.

In 2009, Allison Jones won the women's standing skier super combined event at the US Adaptive Alpine Nationals.

Paralympics emphasize the athletes' achievements rather than their disability.

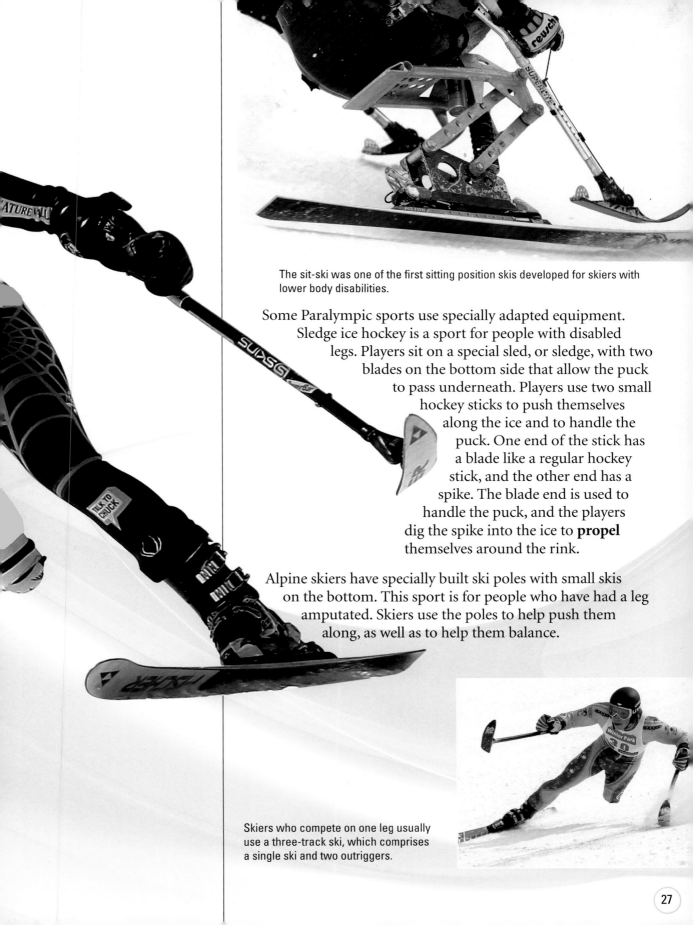

The sit-ski was one of the first sitting position skis developed for skiers with lower body disabilities.

Some Paralympic sports use specially adapted equipment. Sledge ice hockey is a sport for people with disabled legs. Players sit on a special sled, or sledge, with two blades on the bottom side that allow the puck to pass underneath. Players use two small hockey sticks to push themselves along the ice and to handle the puck. One end of the stick has a blade like a regular hockey stick, and the other end has a spike. The blade end is used to handle the puck, and the players dig the spike into the ice to **propel** themselves around the rink.

Alpine skiers have specially built ski poles with small skis on the bottom. This sport is for people who have had a leg amputated. Skiers use the poles to help push them along, as well as to help them balance.

Skiers who compete on one leg usually use a three-track ski, which comprises a single ski and two outriggers.

Olympics and the Environment

Hosting so many people in one city can be costly to the environment. Host cities often build new venues and roads to accommodate the Games. For example, a great deal of transportation is needed to support construction projects, planning for the games, and to move the athletes, participants, volunteers, media, and spectators around the host city and its surrounding areas. This transportation causes pollution.

In recent years, the IOC and Olympic host cities have been working to make the Olympics more green. With their beautiful surroundings, including the Pacific Ocean to the West and the Rocky Mountains to the East, Vancouver and Whistler have taken many steps to protect the environment.

As host city of the 2010 Winter Olympics, Vancouver is taking measures to reduce harmful effects to the environment.

WHISTLER SLIDING CENTRE

At the Whistler Sliding Centre, home to the bobsleigh, luge, and skeleton events, an ice plant is used to keep the ice frozen. The heat waste from this plant is used to heat other buildings in the area. All wood waste from the Whistler sites will be chipped, composted, and reused on the same site.

LIL'WAT ABORIGINAL NATION

Working with the Lil'wat Aboriginal Nation, builders of the Olympic cross-country ski trails created venues that could be used long after the Olympics. About 50 kilometres of trails have been built that can be used by cross-country skiers and hikers of all skill levels.

VANCOUVER LIGHTING AND HEATING SYSTEMS

Venues in Whistler and Vancouver have been equipped with efficient lighting and heating systems. These systems reduce the amount of **greenhouse gases** released into the atmosphere during the Olympics.

GREENHOUSE GASES

Half of the organizing committee's vehicles are either **hybrid** or equipped with fuel management technology. These vehicles emit less greenhouse gases than other vehicles. As well, venues have been made accessible to users of transit, and many event tickets include transit tickets to promote mass transportation at the games.

VANCOUVER CONVENTION AND EXHIBITION CENTRE

The Vancouver Convention and Exhibition Centre uses a seawater heating system. This system uses the surrounding natural resources to make the building a more comfortable place to visit. The centre also houses a fish habitat.

RICHMOND OLYMPIC OVAL

The Richmond Olympic Oval was built with a wooden arced ceiling. The huge amount of wood needed to build the ceiling was reclaimed from forests that have been destroyed by mountain pine beetles. These beetles feed on pine trees, killing them in the process. Using this wood helps stop other, healthy trees from being cut down for construction materials.

🍁 **CANADIAN TIDBIT** The 2010 Games are estimated to cost more than $4 billion, including about $2.5 billion of taxpayer money.

Putting Aerodynamics to the Test

Downhill skiers speed down a hill that is covered in snow and ice. They can reach speeds higher than 100 kilometres per hour as they weave through the gates that make the course. To gain the most speed, skiers hold their bodies in a position called the "tuck." They curl their body and tuck their arms in close to the body. The tuck position makes the skiers more aerodynamic, meaning that air flows around their body more easily. Since the air flows around the body, it creates less resistance. Try this experiment to help you understand aerodynamics.

What you need
an electric fan

1. Stand in front of the fan as it blows air at you.

2. Hold out your hand with your palm facing the fan. The force of the air pushing against your hand is wind resistance. Notice how much force the wind puts on your outstretched hand.

3. Next, make a fist. Do you notice a difference in the way the air hits your fist?

4. Now, hold your fingers together with your fingertips pointing toward the fan. What do you notice about the force of the air on your hand?

5. Imagine you are a skier. How is the tuck position better for skiers than standing straight up with their arms out to the side?

Further Research

Visit Your Library

Many books and websites provide information on alpine skiing. To learn more about alpine skiing, borrow books from the library, or surf the Internet.

Most libraries have computers that connect to a database for researching information. If you input a key word, you will be provided with a list of books in the library that contain information on that topic. Nonfiction books are arranged numerically, using their call number. Fiction books are organized alphabetically by the author's last name.

Surf the Web

If you want to learn more about alpine skiing in Canada, you can explore **www.canski.org**.

To learn more about alpine skiing, visit **www.faqs.org/sports-science/Sc-Sp/Skiing-Alpine.html**.

Glossary

aerobics: exercise for the heart and lungs

aerodynamic: reducing the amount of drag from air resistance

amateur: an athlete who does not receive money for competing

amputee: a person who has had a body part removed

biathlon: a sport in which athletes combine cross-country skiing and target shooting skills

calories: units of energy, especially in food

cerebral palsy: a condition that typically causes impaired muscle coordination

core: the trunk of the body, including the hips and torso

disciplines: subdivisions within a sport that require different skills, training, or equipment

endurance: the ability to continue doing something that is difficult

goalball: a sport for blind athletes that has bells inside the ball

greenhouse gases: gases that trap the Sun's energy in Earth's atmosphere, causing the greenhouse effect

heart rate: the number of times the heart beats in one minute

hybrid: a vehicle that uses a combination of fuels

intellectual disability: a disability that hampers the function of the mind

iron: a substance in foods that is good for the blood

nordic: Olympic disciplines involving cross-country skiing or ski jumping

perseverance: a commitment to doing a task despite challenges that arise in the process

propel: push or cause to move in a particular direction, usually forward

protein: a substance needed by the body to build healthy muscles

Scandinavia: the area of northern Europe containing the countries of Denmark, Norway, and Sweden

spinal cord: a bundle of nerves held inside the spine, connecting almost all parts of the body to the brain

visual impairment: not being able to see well

Index